LITTLE TOOT

By HARDIE GRAMATKY

⌒ **THE CLASSIC ABRIDGED EDITION** ⌒

Illustrated by Mark Burgess

Grosset & Dunlap, Publishers

This book is a presentation of Atlas Editions, Inc. For more information
about Atlas Editions book clubs for children write to:
Atlas Editions, Inc., 4343 Equity Drive, Columbus, Ohio 43228.
Weekly Reader is s registered trademark of Weekly Reader Corporation.

Reprinted by arrangement with Grosset & Dunlap, a member of Penguin
Putnam Books for Young Readers.

2000 Edition

Printed in the USA

Library of Congress Cataloging-in-Publication Data

Gramatky, Hardie, 1907–
   Little Toot / by Hardie Gramatky ; illustrated by Mark Burgess. — Classic
abridged ed.
      p.   cm.
      Summary: Little Toot the tugboat conquers his fear of rough seas when he single-
handedly rescues an ocean liner during a storm.
      [1. Tugboats Fiction.] I. Burgess, Mark, ill. II. Title.
   PZ7.G7654Lg   1999
   [E]—dc21   99-36541
                                                                              CIP

ISBN 0-448-42072-4

At the foot of an old, old wharf lives the cutest, silliest little tugboat you ever saw. His name is Little Toot, because, blow hard as he would, the only sound from his whistle was a small toot-toot-toot.

But what he couldn't create in sound, Little Toot made up for in smoke. From his chubby smokestack he'd send up a volley of smoke balls.

2

That made Little Toot feel very important. And the flag
at his masthead would dance like the tail of a puppy dog.

Now the river where Little Toot lives is full of ships.
They come from ports all over the world. So there is always
work for tugboats to do, either pushing ships into the
docks to be unloaded or pulling them to the ocean to begin
a new voyage.

Little Toot was right in the middle of it all. His father, Big Toot, is the biggest and fastest tugboat on the river. And as for Grandfather Toot, he is an old sea dog who tells of his mighty deeds on the river.

But Little Toot hated work. He was scared of the wild seas outside the channel. He had no desire to be tossed around or pull ships fifty times bigger than himself. He preferred the calm water of the river, where he could always find plenty of fun.

Like gliding, for example...

Or playing thread-the-needle around the piers...

Or cutting figure 8's. Little Toot loved making really big figure 8's.

Little Toot's antics annoyed the hard-working tugboats awfully. One day he made a figure 8 so big it took up the whole river. There was no room at all for a big tug named J. G. McGillicuddy who was bound downstream. He had little love for other tugboats and a frivolous one like Little Toot made him mad.

The other tugboats saw what happened and they made fun of him, saying he only knew how to play.

Poor Little Toot. He was ashamed and angry, but there was nothing he could do about it except blow those silly smoke balls.

Little Toot hid alongside the wharf and sulked. Then he saw a great ocean liner headed down the river. Pulling it were four tugboats, with his own father Big Toot right up in front.

All of a sudden, a great idea burst over him. He *wouldn't* be a silly, frivolous little tugboat any more. He would work like the best of them. He would make Big Toot proud of him. Full of ambition, Little Toot started downstream.

He sidled hopefully up to one big ship after another, tooting
for them to heave a towline. But they supposed he was still
only a nuisance and would have nothing to do with him.

Oscar, the Scandinavian, rudely blew steam in his face....

But the rudest of all was a great transatlantic liner.
It blasted him right out of the water!

That was too much for Little Toot. He wasn't wanted anywhere or by anyone. He was so *lonesome*. Floating aimlessly downstream, he grew sadder and sadder. He didn't even notice the sky had grown dark and the wind was whipping up into a real storm.

Suddenly he heard a sound that was like no sound he had ever heard before. It was the *Ocean*. And the noise came from the waves as they dashed and pounded against the rocks.

But that wasn't all. Against the black
sky climbed a brilliant, flaming rocket.

When Little Toot looked hard, he saw,
jammed between two huge rocks, an
ocean liner. What a terrible thing to see!

Little Toot went wild with excitement. He began puffing those silly balls of smoke out of his smokestack. And then, a wonderful thought struck him. Why, those smoke balls could probably be seen 'way up the river, where his father and grandfather were. So he puffed a signal.

'Way up the river they saw it. Of course they had no idea who was making the signals, but they knew it meant "come quickly." So they all raced to the rescue.

Just in time, too, because Little Toot, still puffing out
his S.O.S., was hard put to stay afloat. One wave spun him
around. Another tossed him up high. Out of the corner of
his eye, when he was hung on a wave, Little Toot saw the
fleet wasn't able to make headway against such fierce seas.

Little Toot was scared green. But *something* had to be
done.

The fleet was on the verge of giving up when suddenly, above the storm, they heard a familiar toot....

It was Little Toot! Not wasting his strength butting the waves as they had done. But bouncing from crest to crest, like a rubber ball. The pounding hurt like everything, but Little Toot kept right on going.

Looking through his binoculars, Big Toot
saw the great vessel throw a line to Little Toot.
When the line was made fast, Little Toot waited
for a long moment....

And then, when a huge wave swept under
the liner, lifting it clear of the rocks, Little Toot
pulled with all his might. *The liner came free!*

The people on board began to cheer.... And the whole tugboat fleet insisted on Little Toot's escorting the great boat back into the harbor. Little Toot was a hero! And Grandfather Toot blasted the news all over the river.

Well, after that, Little Toot became quite a different fellow. He even changed his tune....

And it is said that he can haul as big a load
as his father can...

...that is, when Big Toot hasn't a very big load to haul.